MUPPET BABIES

Kermit the Hermit

CARNIVAL

Carnival
An imprint of the Children's Division
of the Collins Publishing Group
8 Grafton Street, London W1X 3LA

First published by Weekly Reader Books, Columbus, Ohio, USA.
Published by Carnival 1988

ISBN 0 00 194444 4

Printed & bound in Great Britain by
PURNELL BOOK PRODUCTION LIMITED
A MEMBER OF BPCC plc

It was spring-cleaning time in the nursery
  room,
And nothing was safe from the dust mop and
  broom.
Nanny had hired a house-cleaning crew
To make the whole nursery shiny and new.

They shampooed the furniture, dusted the
    toys,
And filled the whole room with confusion
    and noise.
Kermit had nowhere to read or to play.
He wished that the strangers would just go
    away.

"Too many people!" thought poor little
 Kermit.
"Life would be better if I were a hermit!"

A hermit is someone who lives all alone
In a cave with no furniture, TV, or phone.

There's nobody there, so it's peaceful and
  quiet—
"That's just what I want," figured Kermit. "I'll
  try it."

So he scrunched up his eyes and let his
thoughts wander
To an empty old cave in the hills way up
yonder,
An echoing cavern with no one in sight.
"Now I'll be a hermit!" he said with delight.

He got a big stick, and he grew a long beard,
For hermits, thought Kermit, should look a
bit weird.

He crawled through the cave – every crook,
  nook, and cranny.
There was nobody there – no house-
  cleaners, no Nanny,
No one to talk to, no friends big or small,
No playmates to play with, no people at all.
It was *too* calm and quiet. There was nothing
  to do.
He needed excitement – a stranger or two!

Skrinch! came a sound which startled poor
  Kermit.
And up through the floor popped a worm
  named McDermott.

"I bring you good news," said the worm.
   "Pay attention –
Your cave is the site of a hermit convention.
And you shall be chairman of all the great
   hermits,
And give out the prizes and hermitting
   permits."

"I'll do it!" said Kermit politely but proudly.
Just then someone knocked on the door
rather loudly.

"Is this Kermit's cave?" called an old hermit crab.
Then he sat on a boulder and started to gab.

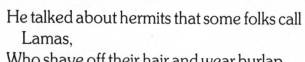

He talked about hermits that some folks call
   Lamas,
Who shave off their hair and wear burlap
   pyjamas.
A Lama in pyjamas is a wonderful sight.
They preen and they prance and can
   dance all through the night.

Just as he mentioned them, several walked in,
Singing and making a glorious din!

The crab then told Kermit of hermits called
    Monks,
Who sleep on the mountain in creaky old
    bunks,
And live on a diet of sausage and ham,
And paste little labels on bottles of jam.

Just as Old Crabby had mentioned their
    name,
Into that cavern the merry Monks came,
Carrying poles (for they do love to shinny 'em),
Converting the cave to a Monk
    condominium.

New hermits walked in – they were young
    ones called Rookies,
Munching and lunching on fresh hermit
    cookies.

They tasted so good they needed some more
  of 'em
But luckily the Rookies had quite a big store
  of 'em.

Beachcombing hermits brought barrels of
   sand.
Hermits with horns formed an all hermit
   band.

Together they made music as if on a beach,
They played so loudly it prevented all
    speech.

Hermits kept coming – more hermits – then
   more!
They could hardly all fit through that little
   cave door.
Hermits with pets and hermits in pairs,
Small hermit turtles and big hermit bears.

They all sat together, as good as could be,
Until they all felt it was time for some tea.

But still there came more from all points of
the compass
Until Kermit wondered if he could stand all
the rumpus.

Hermits with feathers and hermits who
   sneezed.
Hairy old hermits who did as they pleased.
Fat ones and skinny ones, all shapes and
   sizes,
Danced up to Kermit for permits and prizes.

He was writing so fast he thought his hand
  must break,
And by now he was having difficulty staying
  awake.

The cave was so full, Kermit had to cry,
  "Stop!"
And just as he did, his dream broke with a
  pop!

The cave disappeared. He was back in his
  room
With Nanny, the cleaners, the dust mop, and
  broom.

How cosy it seemed after all the commotion.
He looked on it now as if in slow motion.

But now that his hermit adventure was done,
He knew that a big noisy crowd could be fun.

He'd remember it next time when things
became busy
And not be so silly and get in a tizzy.
So he grabbed up a broom and helped out
like a friend.
"I'm proud of you, Kermit," said Nanny . . .

. . . THE END.